Firefly

Firefly

A Miller Creek Saga

PREQUEL

HOLLIS WYNN

Firefly
A Miller Creek Saga Prequel

Copyright © 2021 by Hollis Wynn

Editor: Missy Borucki
Proofreader: C.M. Albert
Cover Design and Formatting: Alt 19 Creative

And if love be madness, may I never find sanity again.
—JOHN MARK GREEN

Fallon

ONE YEAR.

THAT'S HOW LONG it's been since I've set my eyes on Ford and Jameson. Three-hundred sixty-five long days. Considering we live in different states, we rotate who chooses the location for a weekend away once a year. Last year, Jameson picked the beach in Florida. The year before, Ford chose the mountains in Colorado. This year, we're spending a weekend in Miller Creek, Texas, in the heart of the Texas Hill Country.

When I was in college, I couldn't have imagined that in the last six months of being there, I'd fall in love with not only one man, but two.

"Same time next year?" I ask Ford and Jameson as we lay in my bed, legs intertwined, utterly and totally spent.

When I met these guys last year, there was no way I could have imagined this day would come. I planned one last dinner with them before we all go our separate ways. Mitchellson College will forever hold fantastic memories—including the first time I fell in love with two guys.

"Sure. Whatever you say." Ford pulls me closer, and I kiss him on the chest.

"Hey! What about me?" Jameson says, a loud chuckle escaping his throat.

"Well, then scoot in," I respond to him. "I like being the middle of this sexy sandwich."

Jay scoots closer to me, wrapping his arm around my hips and pulling me close as I lay one leg over Ford.

It's not the most comfortable place to be physically, but my heart beats in rhythm with theirs, and it's exactly what I need.

"Yes," Jay answers my question. "Same time next year. No matter what happens while we're apart, we will be together one weekend a year."

I'd fantasized about being with two men before I met them—and it was nothing but spectacular the first time. Each time it gets better and better because when we are together, I am their sole focus. Every look, caress, or touch is all about me.

Five years later, we've met up one weekend every year to remind ourselves of the love we have for each other. During the days we're apart, we make every effort to stay in touch, and we do it well, from calls to texts to video chats. We do whatever it takes to keep in contact. When you love someone, distance often makes the heart grow fonder, and it's true with these guys.

Often I dream of what it would be like to come home from a long day working to a glass of wine waiting, the tub steaming and full of bubbles, and being worshiped from head to toe.

Yes, that's what I fantasize about. And you know what? I own it. Sex is a natural part of life, even though my ultra-conservative parents never discussed it with me. Now that I'm an adult living on my own, they don't have any ownership over me—or my body.

Standing outside the old-fashioned, white clapboard house, I fall in love with the place I rented for the weekend. There's an enormous wrap-around porch with a bed hanging from thick ropes at one end and two wicker chairs with a table in between on the other and bordered by giant ferns hanging from the rafters. No doubt the guys and I will make good use of that swing.

The black shutters frame the windows, and there are multi-colored pots full of flowers surrounding the house, making it feel super homey and comfortable. It is something out of a storybook.

I push the large black door open and make a mental note to leave a large tip when we leave. The owners have made this weekend so easy. Plus, I didn't have to drag bags and bags of groceries with me because they offered to do the food shopping and leave everything ready for us.

It doesn't take me long to explore the house. It's a small farmhouse with the perfect mix of shades of white and gray, grounded by the rich oak floors and ceiling beams. There is a binder on the bar in the kitchen with all the information about the house. I quickly skim through it and note the instructions to heat the hot tub.

The master bedroom sits tucked behind the kitchen. I set my bag on the bench at the end of the bed, spying a door in the corner that leads outside. This room is simple and clean. A king-sized bed is centered between two floor-to-ceiling windows with sheer white floor-length curtains.

Opening the first door, I see a giant bathtub inside a shower and dual vanities. Exiting the bathroom, I make my way to the patio door, and the smell of fresh cut grass greets me. Spotting the hot tub in the corner, I walk over and turn it on because there is no doubt in my mind, we will end our day there.

I make my way back into the bedroom and slide out of my sandals. Leaving them at the end of the bed, I pad my way to the kitchen for a glass of wine and to start dinner.

The guys should arrive in the next couple of hours, so it will be nice to have dinner ready when they get here.

For these weekends, we each plan something to do outside of the house. If I let them, we wouldn't leave the house at all, and I wouldn't be able to walk for a week after. I cook dinner the first night, and the guys find something for us to do in the area. I know we're going on a hike, which no doubt is Ford's doing. He's always been active and can't stand to lounge around for too long. Jay hasn't shared his plans yet, but I know we will all enjoy whatever it is.

It doesn't take me long to find my way around the kitchen. The organized pantry has all the things I requested lined up on one side with paper products and cleaners on the other. Glancing around, I notice an old-fashioned radio. Pulling it out, I place it on the counter and plug it in, allowing the old school country crooners to serenade me.

It doesn't take long for me to lose myself in the chopping, dicing, and marinating process. The smell of cilantro permeates the room, and I sneak a taste of the pico de gallo I've been making.

"Yummy," I mumble to myself. Fajitas is one of my favorite meals, and I know the guys love Mexican, so it's perfect for us. While the meat marinates in the fridge, I toast the rice, then add tomatoes to simmer together, allowing the flavors to meld perfectly.

When we have our weekends away, it's easy to wonder what it would be like to be with them all the time—not having to hide this side of myself. Don't get me wrong, I'm not ashamed of these feelings, but I also don't advertise them.

My father is one of the top lawyers in Houston, and my mother runs a charity for domestic violence victims. They would lose their shit if they thought I would live openly in a romantic relationship with two men. That's why, instead, we meet once a year and make our wildest fantasies a reality. Then we return to our homes, going through the motions of life until we're together again.

I'm so lost in my own world that I don't hear the door open. When Ford walks into the small kitchen and spins me around, I scream in surprise.

I come face-to-face with Ford's beautiful honey-colored eyes before trying to hit him while he attacks my mouth with the ferocity of a man starved. Ford shows his love through physical touch, and I'm totally on board with it. There is something about how he always pulls me into his body and kisses me with abandon, which makes my heart skip a beat.

He crushes me to his body, his tongue dancing with mine. That kiss sends shivers of desire down my spine. Ford's lips are demanding yet soft at the same time. It's been so long since I've been able to lose myself in a kiss that I don't want it to end. Abruptly we both step apart, taking a deep breath, trying to come back down to earth.

I step back, dazed. My heart pounds in my chest, and my legs are as solid as jelly. "I guess we're not waiting on Jay."

"Since when have I ever waited for anything?" He wiggles his eyebrows at me. The irony in his statement isn't lost on me because Ford was never on time for anything in college. He marched to the beat of his own drum, which included never paying attention to the clock.

Then I laugh. Hard. Bending over at the waist, I wheeze, and it feels so good.

Standing straight up, I step back and bump into the counter. "When will..." I pause when I hear the crunch of gravel and step around Ford before running to the front door. I stop and turn to him to say, "Now apparently," before winking and running out the door, down the stairs to Jameson who's unfolding his large body out of a sports car.

"Jay!" I squeal and throw myself into his arms.

"How's my Firefly?" he asks as he hugs me hard.

I peel myself off him and lock eyes, swimming in the pools of melted chocolate that are all mine.

Glancing back at the porch, Ford is leaning against a post, ankles crossed with a smirk on his face. I love that he is okay with letting all his emotions out when he's with us because, as a DEA agent who's badass, he has to hide that part of himself.

"Let's get this party started," I say.

O NCE A YEAR, the three of us get together, locking ourselves away from the rest of the world. It's the best weekend of the year—every year.

Why, you ask?

Because polite southern society doesn't allow three people to be in love with each other, though that's never stopped us, we just do it in private. Jay and I are ready to worship—Fallon—body, mind, and soul.

This isn't what I imagined when I fell head over heels in love with her in college. None of us did. But instead of fighting it, we decided to let it happen.

Until I realized...

Fallon Winters is the one for me.

I must breathe her soul into my heart.

She is my forever.

I watch her with Jay as they walk toward the house, and I wonder what it would be like if she could be mine—ours—all the time.

Fallon

"**D**INNER IS ALMOST ready. All you need to do is heat the outside grill."

"Sounds good," Jay pipes up. "What's for dinner?" He walks to the fridge, grabbing a couple of beers, and pops the tops before handing one to Ford.

I turn around and face him. "Fajitas with all the fixings."

He smiles, and my heart beats a little faster. Jay is and always has been the softer of the two. He's in touch with his emotions and freely shows me his heart. Ford is kind and loving, but he prefers to show affection with his tongue instead of his heart.

Jameson is my emotional lover, while Ford loves my body. Together they take care of both sides of my needs.

"And..." I say, pausing for effect. "I already turned on the hot tub for dessert."

Ford high fives Jay, and they head out to find the grill and get the fire going, though *my* fire is already burning.

Dinner is delicious, and like every year, we easily fall into comfortable conversation. Flirtation and innuendo compete for attention. Ford unabashedly turns each topic back to sex while Jay digs deeper, asking how our lives are.

With full bellies and simmering attraction and need just below the surface of our casualness, I send the guys to the living room to relax while I clean the kitchen. It's an opportunity to center myself before what I know is to come.

"Anyone up for a dip in the hot tub?" I ask them from the doorway, wineglass in hand and a knowing smile on my face. Both turn my way, but I don't wait for a response. "I'll meet you out there."

I grab my bag and head into the bathroom to change. I pull out my favorite navy-striped string bikini and quickly pull on my swimsuit before making my way to the hot tub and slipping into the steaming water, allowing it to soothe my exhausted body.

The sun has set, and I notice a string of outdoor lights around the perimeter of the porch and plug them in for a bit of ambiance. I settle myself into the hot tub and glance out at the edge of the woods, and I notice fireflies dancing in the bushes. I don't see them much in the city, and I catch myself smiling, thinking of Jay.

I lay my head back and close my eyes, allowing the water's warmth to relax my body while my mind wanders.

A little later, the guys stroll out of the house, towels wrapped around their hips, each holding a beer, and Ford has another glass of wine for me.

"Aren't you the sweetest," I say as he hands me the glass, taking the empty and putting it on the table behind us.

Ford smirks at me before dropping his towel and climbing in with me. I sit with my mouth hanging wide open before Jay does the same thing.

"Well then…" is all I can say, knowing this night is about to heat up.

The guys sit beside me—Ford on the left, Jay on the right. Our legs immediately intertwine. I lay my head back on the side of the tub and allow myself to let go of everything from life—no responsibilities or worries. I simply feel. Jay sets his beer and my wineglass on the edge before pulling me into his lap. Ford reaches for my feet, placing them in his lap. With one hand, he presses his thumb into the arch of my foot, causing me to moan from how good it feels. My hips lift off Jay's lap, but he grasps onto them and pulls me back down, securing me to him.

Tilting my head back, Jay takes the invitation, pressing his lips to mine. His tongue searches while he pulls my hair from its bun, letting it float on top of the water.

While Jay makes love to my mouth, Ford pulls at the strings of my bikini bottom, untying them, and they float away.

Damn, these guys aren't wasting any time.

"I love you, Firefly," Jay whispers as he pulls his lips away from mine.

Reaching around and clasping my hands behind his neck, I softly reply, "I love you too."

My whole being is filled with desire. I want both guys to give me exactly what I need—them.

Us.

Touching.

Together.

Forever.

Jameson

I'VE LOVED FALLON since the first day I met her. She's beautiful inside and out.

Kindness radiates from her pores.

A light in the dark.

My Firefly.

There are times in our lives where we're going through the motions, looking for something in the future. That's the way it was when I met Fallon. I wasn't searching for a woman; I was only looking forward to graduation and what would come next.

The moment I opened the door to her standing at the threshold, I couldn't have imagined that this would be our future.

Ford

CALL ME A voyeur if you like, but there is something about watching the two of them kissing, touching, whispering sweet nothings that makes me want her even more.

I believe there can't be another woman who acknowledges and accepts her love for two men as easily as she does. Fallon takes care of those around her and doesn't put up with shit from anyone—including me.

The moment I met her, she took my breath away. I opened my apartment door, and there she stood—the tutor assigned to help me graduate, looking more like a Baywatch babe than a woman who could teach me about criminal justice. She was wearing blue jean shorts that showed off her long tan legs and a tank top that drew my eyes right to her breasts. She hid her clear blue eyes behind huge black sunglasses and piled her long blond hair on the top of her head in a bun.

And then she opened her mouth to yell at me, having no idea how sensual her voice sounded.

But my dick sure did and rose to attention. And I slammed the door in her face. Gray sweats don't hide a cock anytime, much less when it wants to jump out and play.

I should have apologized and talked to her, but I didn't. Instead, I yelled for my roommate Jameson to come and deal with her.

A beautiful woman standing on my doorstep, pissed off and ready to battle, automatically turned me on. It's a day I'll never forget. That day became the most significant day of my life to date. It's the day I met the woman I will marry.

I snap out of my trip down memory lane and take a long swig of my beer before returning to massaging Fallon's feet and legs. There is something about touching her, feeling soft silky skin below my calloused fingers, that relaxes me, letting the stress fall from my body.

I watch her writhe as I massage her feet and up her calves. I slide closer so she doesn't slip under the water as she loses herself in our touch.

Her bikini bottom floats around in the bubbling water, and I watch the sun dip below the horizon. The sky is lit up in shades of oranges and pinks with dark clouds rolling in, creating a beautiful line of demarcation between dark and light.

Much like the three of us.

Fallon is our light.

Jay brings us hope.

Me, I'm the darkness that tries to maneuver between the two.

It's easier to live in the dark. Ignoring the good that is possible with the reality of what exists around us all. It made my decision to be a federal agent even easier. I honed my investigative skills and used them to find criminals. The ones who live underground are the ones I crave finding, though some think that shining the light on them will allow them to not be seen as the bad seeds they are. Fortunately, I work with some great men and women who are aces at teaching these folks otherwise.

Considering my job is all-consuming—yes, I'm a workaholic, but my team knows not to bother me. It's three days once a year that I'm unreachable. Unattainable for anyone other than Fallon. Nothing matters more to me than showing Fallon what she means to me, even if it's only for one weekend.

Jay sits up, pulls the string behind her neck, and the force of the water sweeps up the triangle top. He immediately unties the string on her back, and the top is gone. Her magnificent body is on display for us—and only us.

My cock lengthens as she wiggles around. Taking advantage of her ass sitting so close to me, I allow my hand to trail up her legs and into the promised land. I slide one finger into her hot wet pussy, then two. With my other hand, I push her hips more toward the surface and begin placing kisses over her abdomen.

One kiss.

Two kiss.

Three kiss.

I keep going until I reach her navel. Lifting my head, I wink at her while working my fingers deeper and deeper into her body. She bucks her hips hard, and I feel Jay moving and then clasping his hands onto her ass, holding her still.

I move my fingers in a "come-hither" motion and stroke her clit with my thumb. She moans loudly, and Jay leans over, capturing the sounds with a kiss. I love her moans and groans of pleasure, but what I want more is her surrender. It's time to move this party to the bedroom.

Before the night is over, we will be one.

All three of us.

Fallon

STANDING IN THE darkened bedroom, dripping wet from the hot tub, I can feel the animal magnetism between us. Ford is so self-confident and doesn't question whether I love him. Jay is quiet and calm, unlike Ford's demanding alpha-like tendencies. Each one feeds a piece of my soul, allowing me to feel loved and worshiped on every front.

Never have I wondered if the guys were attracted to each other or if they wanted someone else. Tonight, more than ever, I can see it in their eyes that they're only focused on me.

"Are you ready?" Ford asks.

He's seen me naked dozens of times, but as his whiskey-colored eyes rake over every inch of my skin, I feel seen, loved, and desired like never before. The heat mirrored at me when his eyes pin mine sends shivers of anticipation to every sensitive part of my body. Every nerve ending is on fire, and I know there is only one way to satisfy the craving that's slowly pooling between the soft curve of my thighs.

I nod because my mouth feels dry, and words escape me as I glance between them. They're both so different, and yet, exactly what my body and heart need at this moment.

Jay grabs my hand, and then we follow Ford into the bathroom. I step around them and turn the shower on to steaming hot. Ford steps up behind me and pushes my hair away before nibbling on my neck.

The steam from the shower billows out, and I pull away laughing because Ford knows I'm ticklish in that spot. I step into the shower, my back to the water, allowing it to beat on my neck. The guys step in with me. Ford blocks the water with his large frame as he maneuvers behind me. Jameson kisses me, sliding his hand past me, grasping the shower gel.

The guys wash me from the top of my shoulders to the bottom of my feet. I do my best to keep my hair from getting wet because I don't want to take the time to dry it.

We exit the shower, and Jay towels me off before taking the time to dry himself. Ford dries himself and then opens the door and leads me into the bedroom to the bed.

Jay follows us, pulling the club chair from the corner, facing it toward the bed. Keeping his eyes on mine, I watch him as he props his leg up on the end of the bed and begins stroking himself.

My tongue slips between my lips, yearning to replace his hand with my mouth. I fixate my eyes on the movement of his hand—up and down and slipping over the crown of his hardness. Completely lost in the moment, I don't immediately feel Ford behind me until his hands run along my sides, goose bumps peppering my skin as they glide from my hips to my torso. His arms wrap around me, large rough palms cup my breasts, kneading them gently. My eyes fall shut as I relax into him and lose myself in the feeling of his fingers as they flick and tug one of the most sensitive erogenous zones on my body. I squirm in his arms, but he presses one hand against my abdomen, steadying me as the other continues the attention to my breasts. The hand holding me in place slowly lowers to my mons. The motion forces my hips back, and I can feel him hard against me from behind. Ford drops his lips to my neck, nipping and licking. Licking and nipping. It is the sweetest torture.

A moan passes my lips as the gentle sweep of his tongue close to my ear, and the expert tugging of my nipples becomes more assertive, edging me toward the orgasm he knows is building. I swear, the man can make me come with his touch alone.

As if reading my mind, he lowers his hand, his thick fingers parting my already wet folds. "Open your eyes, baby girl. I want you looking at Jay when you come undone."

My eyes fly open, locking my gaze on Jay's kind, dark eyes. Only now, they reflect so much more. Desire and a promise of the way he plans to work over my body when he has a chance. Ford rolls my clit between his fingers while his other hand massages and pinches my nipples—hard. This elicits a soft moan as his tongue lathes my neck, drawing the skin in deep and making my eyes roll back from pleasure.

"I can't," I whimpered on the precipice of my first orgasm. These men know my body better than I do—and know exactly how to please me faster than anyone ever has. "I need to—"

"It's okay, baby girl. You can come for me," Ford whispers in my ear.

As if he could stop me. My back arches, my head falling on the thick, sinewy muscles of his shoulders. The last image in my mind before I explode under Ford's fingers is the way Jay's hand sensually grips his cock, a promise glinting back at me in his sexy, hooded eyes.

I bite down, gripping Ford's hips behind me as he rubs harder, his fingers dipping between my folds to wet his fingertips and roll my swollen bud even faster. When he gently bites my neck, I come undone. My body melts, shuddering as white lights pulse behind my closed lids, and I sink deeper into my first orgasm.

I roll in his arms, searching for the mouth I've memorized and constantly long for. "Ford," I say huskily, biting his lip and drawing it in. He cups my ass and lifts me to his lips, making me yelp. He wastes no time claiming my mouth with his heated, passionate kiss.

Our tongues meet—his is sensual and strong. He always finds a way to take the lead in the bedroom, and I don't mind one bit. My body is still humming, revved and ready to go when I feel Jay behind me, swinging my long blond hair over my shoulder so he can find his favorite kissing spot just behind my ear. I giggle as his lips brush the skin softly, sending goose bumps over my body.

Where Ford is rough and sexy, Jay is smooth and sensual—both gods over my body, just in different ways. Jay knows how to take his time and build my arousal to a crescendo, while Ford demands—pushing me to new limits and heights.

"My turn," Jay says, taking my hand.

Ford pulls back, nipping at my lip one last time. Jay wastes no time finding my lips, branding me with his own sexy charm. His hands slide up my neck, and my body shivers with anticipation. If Ford is a master with his fingers, Jay rivals that skill with his tongue. His hands possessively cup my face, his dark eyes taking me in before lowering his mouth for a kiss.

It's deep and sensual, as if he can't get enough of me and never wants it to end.

I wrap my arms around his waist, finding his lean hips and then sliding my hands over his sculpted ass.

"I've been waiting a long time for you, Firefly."

"I'm worth the wait, right?" I tease.

"You're worth everything." He playfully pushes me back onto the bed, and I can't help but giggle. It dies on my lips though, when I see the heated longing in his eyes.

"Damn, you're beautiful," he says, running his hand up my thigh.

I moved higher on the bed at his urging, his eyes zeroing in on the crevice between my legs. "I want to taste you, Fallon."

Jay gently kisses the firefly tattoo on my hipbone, as he always does. Then he trails his mouth along my stomach and down the inside of my parted legs, his fingers squeezing the soft skin of my upper thighs. I moan, the anticipation of that first flick of his tongue nearly undoing me.

I opened my eyes, which was a mistake. Ford is watching us hungrily, desire burning in his eyes and making them richer, darker—an amber shade of sexual arousal that comes out to play whenever the three of us are together. His hand lowers to his abdomen. I can't take my eyes off him as he traverses his happy trail and finds his thick, swollen shaft.

That's when Jay's soft, warm tongue finds my center. Electricity shoots through me, and my hands instinctively find his thick, long hair. Gripping the tresses, I'm unable to appreciate how soft each strand feels. All my senses are diverted to one place—the apex where Jay's mouth is slowly, sensually kissing me. Worshiping me.

His tongue languidly traces along my opening before flicking gently when he gets to the top. My body spasms as he hits my clitoris just right, my body happily surrendering with each lash of his tongue. He continues to tease, taste, stroke—but my body needs more. Jay knows it too. He can read my body like it's his full-time job. His mouth covers my sensitive bud now, his tongue worshipping it until my thighs shake.

He moans appreciatively, then slides his tongue back along my wet center again.

"More," I gasp.

"I know, Firefly. I know," he breathes. "Patience."

His fingers trail my opening, replacing his tongue. As he kisses and bites and suckles me, his fingers slide into my center. My hips lift of their own accord, pressing closer to his mouth as he makes love to me with his tongue and fingers. My body sings his praises, every sensation overstimulated and ready to burst. My body's grown used to this kind of pleasure now—the raw *need* of being with both men. The only problem is the loss is that much greater when I don't have them.

But Jay doesn't let me dwell in that concern. He presses another finger deep inside me, curling them just so. My thighs grip him as he flicks his tongue faster—the sounds of him loving me, making me wild with lust.

"God, Jay!" I can't take it any longer.

Ford walks over, no longer watching and stroking himself, as he loves to do. I glue my eyes to his as he circles the bed. My insides weep with gratitude because I know that hungry look. And I want nothing more than to answer it. I want to give the man everything tonight. My body. My heart. My soul.

Hell—who am I kidding? They both already have them.

Ford cups my breasts, his mouth covering my nipple and sucking hard. I gasp, my body shaking as it tumbles over the edge, another orgasm slamming into me. The vibrations of Jay's moans add to the intensity of every wave, and he continues to lap at my core as I ride down my high.

Only in the safety of my guys am I able to express myself this way—investigate my desire and surrender to them. It feels scary, vulnerable, and sacred all at once. All I know is, it feels right. My body feels most at home in the safety of their arms.

"You're the only taste I can ever think of, Fallon. The one I crave the most. My god, you taste amazing." I hear Jay say as Ford kisses up my chest and neck, reaching my lips.

"I love you," I whisper to Ford.

"I love you too. You're what keeps me tethered."

We lay there a while longer, our bodies tangled as we catch our breaths. I can't help but smile. Every time I'm with them, it feels like my heart caves a little deeper. And I can tell by the way they both looked at me tonight that they feel the same way.

I need this. I need them.

As we get ready for bed, warmth floods over me as joy fills my heart. It sounds cheesy, even to me, but somehow, the three of us complete each other. We just make sense. There's no jealousy, no rivalry, no competition.

They love me so much. They just want to make me happy.

Mission accomplished.

That night, I fall asleep with a soft, satiated smile on my face. And what did I dream of?

I dreamed of us falling asleep this way together... forever.

Jameson

LAST NIGHT WAS exactly what we needed—all
of us. There is something about our connection
that allows me to relax.

Watching Ford and Fallon together makes me hard.
Even this morning, as I stand here drinking a cup of
coffee watching the sun rise, all I can think about is being
with her. Not just once a year, but every day.

I want to wake up with her beside me or between us
every morning. I want to go to bed with her snuggled up
in my arms. I need to take care of her when she's sick.
People think they have a right to tell others how to live,
and it pisses me off. No one should be allowed to tell
anyone else how to live their life—especially ours. We're
not hurting anyone by loving each other.

The sky has a stunning glow as the sun rises. I finish
my coffee then head into the house to pack our backpacks
for a day hike while they sleep.

I get the bacon in the oven quickly so I can make breakfast tacos to eat while we're out. I fill the travel cups with coffee and chop up some fruit and veggies to take along with granola bars. I add extra water bottles to the pile before I head into the bedroom to wake them up.

"Good morning," I say loudly as I crawl onto the bed and wake Fallon with a kiss. It doesn't take more than a couple of seconds before she's kissing me back. I pull her to my body, rolling over and laying her on top of me.

Ford is moaning and groaning on the other side of the bed. "Quit your grumping and get your ass in the shower," I say to him.

He just mumbles at me before getting up, cock saluting the world, then heading into the bathroom and turning on the shower.

It doesn't matter how old we get, Ford will never be a morning person. From the first time I met him in the dorm in college, he's been a miserable human when he wakes up. It makes me wonder how he ever gets to work on time. But then, I guess when you're a fed, a typical schedule isn't an eight to five.

"You ready for some time in nature?" I ask Fallon as she snuggles into me. "The coffee is ready, but you have to get out of bed for it." I run my fingers up and down the soft skin of her back before popping her on the ass.

"Hey," she screeches in my ear, then laughs.

"Time to get this fine ass moving." She rolls off me and plants her feet on the floor.

"Fine, I'm going to shower with Ford then." Sticking out her tongue at me, she winks and heads into the bathroom, closing the door behind her.

"Damn it," I say to myself. I knew I should have tried to stay in bed longer.

Fallon

I NOTICE AS I dress for a day outdoors that I'm sore from the guys worshipping my body last night. And I love it. I can't explain the way I feel the morning after we spend the night together. My body moves a bit slower, and I feel the remnants of our lovemaking in every muscle. When I am finally dressed in my hiking clothes, otherwise known as yoga pants, long sleeve tee, and sneakers, I head into the kitchen to see if I can help Jameson with anything, but it looks like he's got it all together.

"Well, aren't you Mr. Mom," I quip, and he turns from where he's cleaning the stove and side-eyes me.

I nearly fall over laughing because taking care of others is Jay's love language. It's so nice to have someone who will take care of me instead of me having to take care of them. I love cooking and entertaining, but my family struggles with deciding little things, like what's for dinner. It's exhausting having to make all the decisions at work and when I'm with my family. Thankfully, I have my own place, but you'd never know it because the minute I walk into my parents' house, they stop making decisions. It's the oddest dynamic I've ever experienced.

When I'm with the guys, it's nice to have someone expecting my needs. Although I don't need someone to take care of me, I can't deny how great it feels when it's Jay or Ford making me their priority.

"Everything is ready. Just need to grab the backpacks," he tells me.

"Where's Ford?" I ask.

"He's cleaning out his truck so we can take it. I have no idea how it's such a wreck since he's only driven from the airport to here."

Ford is a clean freak in most aspects of his life, but when it comes to a vehicle, he's a disaster—always has been, I'm sure always will be.

"Ahh, gotcha. Some things never change," I laugh and open my backpack to start loading it up with everything we need: sunscreen, water, snacks, bug spray, and wipes.

He loads up the other two packs, and we head out hand in hand for a day of fun in the sun.

The drive to Enchanted Rock doesn't take long, and we spend the time catching up on all the things that have happened in the last year.

"My sister got married a couple of months ago. I'm so glad it's over. For almost a year, all I heard was my mother bitching because Indy was a Bridezilla and wanted everything her way. I don't know how many times I told Mom that she was the Motherzilla because it was Indy's wedding, and she should have what she wanted," Ford says.

"I swear, if I ever get married, I'm going to just elope. I can't imagine how awful my mom would be, and I can't take it. She'd want me to have the best wedding ever, but she's also a socialite and would want to invite all of Houston society. No way!"

"You want to get married?" Jay asks, glancing over at me. His voice is thick and unsteady, which shocks me. His eyes dart toward Ford, then back to me.

"I do. I know that if we stay together, that it won't be a traditional wedding because of antiquated laws and such." I shrug my shoulders. "But yeah, I'd love to wear a white dress and get married at sunset."

As soon as the words are out, my heart skips a beat. I want to marry these men. I want to be with them forever, but I have no idea how it would work.

"Do you guys want to get married?" I ask them, my voice shaking. The door is already open, so I might as well walk through it.

Jay is the first to respond, and I'm not shocked by that. "Absolutely."

Ford is slower to reply. "I haven't really thought about it. Mostly because I don't know how it would work."

He's not wrong about that. There is only one way that I can picture this working and that is if I was legally married to one and had a commitment ceremony with the other. Then we'd have to have a large home, with a smaller one on a large parcel of property. At some point, we'd have to tell our families, but we would need to be discreet until then.

"All I know is when I imagine what my wedding looks like, it's the three of us. If I can't have both of you, I don't want anyone."

The truck goes silent, no one saying a thing. I'm sure they're both lost in their own heads, much like I am.

I watch the landscape change from fields of wildflowers and grapes to the old school town of Fredericksburg, and now the rise of Enchanted Rock comes into view.

As much as I would love to discuss our future together, I can feel the tension my declaration has created. It's a topic we will leave for another time. For now, it's about us being together.

Ford

THIS IS THE last thing I thought we'd be talking about this weekend. Marriage. Three. I'd love to be married to her, and I can unequivocally say I don't want to be married to Jay. He is my best friend, but I don't want to be with him that way.

When we were in college and chatting about how much we both loved Fallon, it was easy. I'm sure Fallon thought about a future with both of us or one of us, but I didn't. All I thought about was how much I loved her and that I wanted to be with her. When Jay said he adored her and wanted to be with her also, we came to an agreement.

I'm sure there are moments when we wondered if we were all bat shit crazy, but the reality is it works for us. There are times we've each been with Fallon alone too. It is how we've always been, and I'm okay with it.

All I want is for Fallon to be happy and loved.

Whatever she needs from me, I'll do.

I don't care that her father hates me because I came from a middle-class family. He's a wealthy father who takes his traditions to the extreme. I'm sure he decided when Fallon was born that he would find her the perfect husband. Someone who is rich and can take care of her financially. I wonder if he ever considered that taking care of her heart is just as important as money, if not more.

It makes me crazy that it's been five years since we graduated, and she still works for him. I'm sure he's offered her a ton of money to help him at the office. Fallon has always had money because he is a good provider, but the one thing she doesn't have is the ability to tell him no when he asks for help.

Her father is one manipulative son of a bitch, and I hate him for it.

Right after we graduated, Fallon invited me to come to Houston to visit her, and who was I to tell her no. I booked a hotel close to her parents' house where she was living at the time. We spent most of the weekend bumming around town and hanging out by their pool.

It wasn't until after dinner on Sunday night when her father took me to his study and began questioning me. Where was I from? Did I have a job? What was I going to do with the rest of my life?

I knew right then he would never deem me good enough for his little girl. I was correct in that assumption.

When I told him I had applied to be a special agent at the Drug Enforcement Administration, he laughed in my face, then pulled his checkbook out of the oversized wooden desk that took up most of the room.

I watched him write out a check and hand it over to me. I glance down at the check—one hundred thousand dollars, from the account of Arison Trust.

Shaking my head, I refused the check. "I'm sorry, sir. I can't take this."

"You can, and you will. My daughter deserves better than someone like you."

Instead of arguing with him, I folded the check and put it in my pocket, planning to show Fallon before I left. Only, I didn't want to lose her, so I kept quiet.

The next day I made a copy of the check and placed it in my home safe before opening a new account and depositing the check.

One day I'll tell her about it and figure out what to do with the money. Until then, it continues to earn interest.

Fallon

T HE DAY GOES by in a flash. The giant mound of rocks that rise from the earth are various shades of red with dots of green where the trees plant their roots. The sun beats down on us and it isn't long before I've stripped off my long sleeve shirt, tying it around my waist.

Summer in Texas is never cool, but I'm more used to the humidity in Houston than the drier air that plagues the Hill Country. It is nice that the evenings tend to cool off a bit more here than at home.

Both of the guys are mindful of the heat and make us stop for frequent water breaks. I watch as they walk slightly ahead of me for a few minutes, lost in conversation. It isn't often that we can spend time together in public and watching them, I can see that over the years they've become more than friends. If I didn't know better, I'd think they were brothers.

I watch Jay's body tense as he stops and moves off to the side of the trail, allowing others to pass. None of us planned on having the conversation about marriage, but I'm glad we are. It's important to me that they can come to terms with how I feel. I want to be with them, but only if they're able to be comfortable with the three of us being together. I could never choose between them.

Each year, when I leave them after our weekend together, it gets harder and harder for my heart to heal. My family doesn't hesitate to call me out and ask what's going on. Especially my sister. Farrah may be younger than me in age, but she's much older in spirit. From the time she was born, I remember my grandmother saying she had an old soul. At six years old, that didn't make much sense to me, but now, it's easy to see.

Farrah is the caretaker in our family. She spends time with my mother's chef, learning to make all our favorite foods. She volunteers with a charity that helps teach older people how to read while she is going to college. One day she's going to meet a man whose soul speaks to hers and appreciates her for all she offers.

Me, I've already found that person—persons. Ford and Jameson are my people. My home.

Ford turns and holds his hand out for me to grasp as I walk closer to them. Electricity shoots to my heart as soon as we connect. He pulls me into his chest, and

I lean my head back on his shoulder, opening my neck up to his kisses.

"You're getting awfully pink," Jay says to me.

I groan slightly because the last thing I need is a sunburn, but I don't want to put my shirt back on because it's so hot out.

"Can you spray me down again?" I ask him, stepping out of Ford's embrace.

He nods and swings his backpack off his shoulder, setting it down in front of him. He makes quick work of locating the sunscreen while I set my bag on the ground. Turning away from him, I tip my neck down and allow him to cover my back and neck with sunblock. His firm hands feel soft on my skin, and I take a deep breath, refusing to allow a moan to escape.

A few minutes later, my back, neck, arms, and chest are covered, and we're on our way to the parking lot.

When I was perusing the binder, I noticed a summer market—Second Saturday—where the locals come together, closing off Main Street for the day. Apparently, there's live music and vendors of all types, including local wineries and brewpubs, so Jay decided we would stop on the way back to the house to check it out.

We stop at a food truck named Tacos & Tequila for a late lunch, early dinner. Ford and Jameson stand in line to order while I scope out a picnic table.

Glancing around, I notice cheerleaders selling tickets for some type of fundraiser and a couple of fun games for kids to play. The local restaurants have their doors open and tables lining the sidewalk.

Jay sets down three margaritas on the table, and Ford places a massive tray of tacos in front of us. Ford slides onto the bench across from me, and Jay sits to my left.

"Are you guys planning to feed an army?" I ask them.

"Nope. Just us," Jay quips. "We're hungry guys after all."

I pick up my strawberry margarita, holding it up. "Cheers," I say, and the guys raise their glasses. We clink them together, then I take a long drink of the icy goodness.

"That is so good," I sigh out.

Picking up the first taco, I notice they wrapped each one in a napkin and foil to keep the juices from running all over everything.

I chose what I assume is pork based on the cilantro, onion, and pineapple topping. I take a bite, moaning from the flavor.

"Damn, this is a great taco." Then I take two more bites before finishing it.

"Fallon Marie," Ford says, "you know better than to moan in public."

I lean over, laughing at him, before glancing at Jay sitting next to me with a giant smirk on his face.

"You should stop now unless you want the whole town to see us both kiss you."

"Fine. I'll keep the moans to a minimum."

I'm not ashamed of how I feel about them, but I also don't want to give anyone a reason to call us out. Which is something I need to get over if we're going to make a go of this for real.

We spend the rest of the afternoon walking around the square. The last stop we make is at a tent with hand-made wood carvings. I look at all the unique pieces, picking them up one by one, noticing all the details.

"Fallon, did you see this one?" Jay asks, holding up a small wooden box with a firefly carved in the top.

My eyes light up, and I know I need to have it. I step closer to him, taking the box from his hands, running my fingers through the grooves. I sit the box down on the table, lifting the top. It's the perfect place for a ring or necklace.

"My granddaughter loves fireflies, so I made one for her, and she suggested I make another one to sell. She was certain there was someone in this world who loved fireflies as much as she does."

The smiling older man stands behind the table. He has a head full of white hair and is wearing a blue plaid short-sleeved button-down with jeans.

He's the definition of a doting grandfather. I can't picture my father as a grandparent. The man wears a suit every day of his life, except on Saturday when he wears a polo shirt and khaki pants to play golf.

"Well, she is correct. I love fireflies." I glance at the guys who are standing slightly behind me. "I'll take it."

I pull out the cash I had stuffed in the pocket of my yoga pants, but before I can hand it to the gentleman, Jay has already paid.

The owner looks at me and then at Jay. I shrug, place the cash back in my pocket, and smile.

"Thank you," I say while I watch him wrap the box in paper and place it in a brown paper bag.

"I hope you enjoy it as much as my granddaughter."

I say thank you again, grab Jay's hand, and head back to Ford's truck.

Jameson

THIS DAY HAS been intense. Yeah, I knew from the forecast that the sun would be hot and the temperatures extreme. I anticipated it would take everything out of us physically, but what I didn't expect was the emotional roller coaster of the day.

There were moments when we walked in total silence, oblivious to the surrounding landscape. Fallon's position on marriage and the question about wanting to get married caught me off guard. Yet, I didn't think twice before responding.

She's my Firefly—an effervescent spirit.

The one for whom my heart beats.

Without question, I'll do anything she asks of me.

Now, how do we make this happen?

Fallon

THE MILLION-DOLLAR QUESTION is, what are we going to do? It isn't the first time I've thought about spending my life with these men. But it is the first time I've asked if they wanted to marry me—or anyone at all.

From the day we came together, this question was inevitable—who would be my forever?

I sit on the giant porch swing, wrapped in a cozy blanket, a glass of wine in my hand as I stare out at the property around me. The crickets serenade me with their mating call breaking the silence. It's the classic sign of summer, and I love it.

This would be the perfect place for us to live. We're not that far from town yet isolated enough that we can do whatever we want without prying eyes. I wonder if there is another place around here like this that I could buy? Mentally, I make a note to find a local real estate agent.

"So, are we going to talk about the giant elephant in the room?" Ford asks, leaning on the door frame.

I glance over my shoulder at him and blush. Twisting around, I situate my body in the corner of the swing, watching and waiting for Jay to join us.

"Are we?"

He nods and then grabs a chair from the other end of the porch, bringing it closer to me. Jay comes out and hands Ford a beer before sitting on the other end of the swing and pulls my feet into his lap.

"Let's talk," Jay states, his voice steady and full of conviction.

"I've already made it known I want to be with you guys, but now I need to know how you feel." Pulling the blanket up closer to my face, I realize how nervous I am. My insides are quaking from the uncertainty.

Usually, Jay is the more contemplative one, but this time, it's Ford who sits back, watching, eyes darting from Jay to me.

Instead of jumping in to start the conversation, I wait, allowing them the opportunity to speak when they are ready.

"Look, Firefly," Jay says. "You know I love you. I can't imagine a day when I won't love you, but I'm somewhat uneasy about this."

He pauses, and I know he's trying to find the right words.

"So am I," Ford comments.

Honestly, I'm relieved that they are thinking this through. The last thing I want is for Ford and Jay to agree to something just to make me happy. We all deserve happiness, even if it's not together.

"Look," I say, then stop and close my eyes, trying to hold back the tears. "I know you guys love me, and not once have I doubted that, but I can't continue this way. I can't live waiting for one weekend a year where we can all be together. Praying that you guys aren't with someone else in the meantime."

I wipe away the first tear that drops, and Jay pulls me to him, kissing away the others that fall. Ford moves from the chair to the other side of me. I'm wrapped in a cocoon of their love, yet I can't help but wonder if this will be the last time.

"Firefly, you're the only one I'm with—the only one I want to be with."

I say nothing, just nod.

"Fallon," Ford says, leaning into me and tipping my head up to make eye contact. "As Jay said, I love you. You're my forever. But this isn't a simple decision to make, and you know that."

Ford is correct. It is the most difficult decision we'll ever make.

"I know, but I don't want to look back in twenty years and wonder if I stopped you from falling in love and having a family. Nor do I want that for me."

Wiping at the tears streaming down my face, I don't know what the right thing is. This is the first time I've acknowledged the conflict I feel about this whole thing to them.

"Do you guys love each other or just me? Am I the thing that makes this all work?"

They look at each other, and I can see the wheels turning in their minds. "There isn't a right answer. Just tell me the truth." I say.

"Jay is my best friend. He has been since the first time we met. We had an instant brotherly like bond. But no, I'm not *in love* with him, although I do love him."

I turn slightly and look at Jay.

"Same. There is a bond between us that I can't explain, but no, I don't love him like that," he says, then points at Ford. "But we both love you."

"He's right. But I should point out that I'm totally fine with you loving both of us most of the time. However, sometimes I want you all to myself," Ford says.

"Jay, do you feel the same?" I ask, my voice sounding fragile and shaky, much like my body.

He doesn't answer, just looks at Ford, then nods.

And we're back to square one. "What the fuck do we do now?" I blurt out.

The guys laugh at my brash comment, and I'm thankful for the moment of levity during this crazy time.

"If it were up to me," Ford begins, "we'd buy some property where we could live together for a while and see what happens. However, with us all living in different locations, that's a bit difficult. So maybe we work on getting us all in one place first."

Jay takes a moment, and his response catches me off guard. "I like that idea. I can be a cop anywhere. The challenge is finding a place we might all want to live that Ford can transfer to."

We each nod in silence, the wheels turning. "I'm not married to my job, and one day I'd like to have my own business, but I can do that anywhere."

"Well, it's decided. We will find a place where we all want to live. Any ideas?" Jay asks.

"Austin isn't a bad spot," Ford says. "Houston isn't horrible either, and then Fallon, you wouldn't have to move."

"But what about Jay?" I ask. "Would you be okay with either of those spots?"

"I'd rather be a small-town cop, but if those are your choices, then I'm okay with it. Small towns, though high on drama and Nosey Nelly's, tend to be light on the major crimes, which would allow us to have a better life."

"Houston is fine, but I'm not sure I want to be that close to my parents long term. Plus, the city may be large, but it seems as if everyone knows everyone there, and they are a bunch of... what did you call them? Nosey Nelly's?" I chuckle. Ironically, more often than I'd like, my parents' friends will see me in public and want to talk to me even if I don't know them all that well.

"I think it would be easier to live on our own terms if we start fresh in a place that's new to all of us," Ford comments.

He's not wrong about that. Then we all are on the same foot, and one person doesn't have the advantage.

"I like it here. Maybe not this house particularly, but out here. The town is small, but we're close enough to Austin. We could go into the city, and it's not a major ordeal. Plus, I'm fairly certain there is a DEA office there, too, and maybe Ford could transfer."

"It is nice here," Jay says, "but before we go looking at property, we need to determine what the time frame is going to be for us to try to get jobs in the area."

I watch Ford as he stares into the woods at the other end of the patio. "Is there the chance that there is an opening around here?" I ask him.

"There is always a chance, but even if I transfer, it would be at least six months before I could get here."

Shifting in my seat, I hand Jay the empty wineglass to place on the table next to the swing and curl my legs under me, leaning into Jay. That's not so bad.

"I'm totally on board with this. Next summer, if all the pieces work out, we could celebrate being together forever, instead of just a weekend. What do you think?"

"That works for me," Ford says, smiling at me.

"Me too," Jay responds.

"Then that's it. We have a year to get things in order and find a place we're all comfortable with."

"Deal. Now, I don't want to talk anymore," Ford says, wiggling his eyebrows at us.

He unfolds his long limbs and straightens up the porch before pulling me to my feet and squatting down. I jump on his back like I used to do years ago and laugh while he gives me a piggyback ride into the house, Jay hot on our heels.

We've done so much talking today, and now all I want to do is feel.

Skin to skin.

Heart to heart.

Breaths intermingled, fingers exploring.

We make our way through the house—Jay turning off the lights the as we go—and Ford doesn't stop until we reach the bedroom. The door clicks closed behind us, and I pull off my T-shirt, tossing it to Jay. His face lights up before he dives for the bed—and me.

Tonight, we celebrate us—our love. Our way.

WHEN SHE ASKS for something, I'm hard-pressed to tell her no. Especially when she asks me to love her forever. Even if it means I spend the rest of my life sharing her with Jay. I know that he'll always be gentle with her heart, and if something were to happen to me, she wouldn't be alone.

From the moment she walked into our lives, it was inevitable we would have to decide what our forever looked like.

Now we're there.

Loving Fallon has always been easy. She's the other half of me that I didn't know was missing, and I don't want to imagine life without her.

Here's to forever—our way.

Fallon

"WHAT'S UP, BUTTERCUP? How was your kinky weekend with the guys?" Piper asks the minute she answers the phone.

"Seriously, Pipe?" I respond, laughing at her. "As usual, it was a fabulous weekend."

"Nice. Are you going to spill all the deets, or do I have to wait until we have drinks this week?"

I chuckle because Piper is the best friend a girl could have. We met when we were teenagers and have been thick as thieves ever since. At fourteen, I never could have imagined we'd form a lifelong bond over our love of No Doubt and all things Gwen Stefani. But alas, we did, and she's the only one outside of the guys who knows anything about my annual weekend away.

"If you really want to know—" I begin until she butts in.

"Hell yeah, I want to know all the things. Now."

"Fine," I sigh out. It's not that I don't want to share what transpired with her. My heart beats a bit fast because it's the first time I'm sharing this much of myself with anyone outside of Ford and Jameson.

"Well, we made some big decisions this weekend."

"Oh, what kind of decisions? Tell me everything," Piper says.

I can hear her rummaging around in the fridge. That girl has the metabolism of a cross-country runner, though I don't think she's ever run—except to the fridge for a snack.

"The guys are going to look for jobs around Austin and Miller Creek. We loved the house we stayed at this weekend and have decided that we all want to be together in one place."

"Omigod!" Piper screams, and I immediately turn the volume down in my car. I should have expected it, but man, is her voice shrill when she gets excited. "What exactly does that mean? Are you moving? Are you getting married?"

I interrupt her, or she'll spend the next hour asking questions.

"It means I'm going to be moving to wherever the guys can get jobs in that area. We want to be together, and I am not living close to my parents with two men.

Don't get me wrong, it's not their business, but I don't want to deal with the drama that will come when my dad figures out I'm not marrying the man of his choice."

The traffic in front of me slows down, and I consider pulling over for a soda, but Piper is still peppering me with questions.

"So, who are you going to marry?"

Oh shit. I knew this was coming.

"Look, we don't have all the details worked out yet. We are planning on being in the same place within six months. That means, next year, instead of hiding out for a weekend, we'll be together every night."

"Buttercup, I know this will not be easy for you, but I'm so freaking excited! You're going to have the life you've been dreaming about."

"Thanks, Pipe. It means so much to have you in my court. You know this news will not go over well with my parents, but I'm determined to make it happen. Plan to be available with tissues and alcohol for afterward."

"For sure, I've always got your back!"

"Which is just one thing I love about you. Let me know what day works for dinner and drinks this week."

"I'll check my calendar and get back to you. Be safe," she says and disconnects her phone, my car switching back to the radio.

The traffic starts to flow better, and I decide to take the rest of the trip to figure out how to break the news to my parents.

But no matter what happens, I know Ford and Jameson will be waiting for me with open arms.

If you'd like to see read about what happens
next to Ford, Fallon and Jameson,
you can add *The Rumors are True* to
your Goodreads here: https://bit.ly/HW-TRAT

FORD MACKENZIE.
JAMESON PARKS.

As different as night and day. Yet these two men stole my heart in college, and the three of us forged an unbreakable bond. One that grew stronger year after year.

Our love was a living breathing thing, until two pink lines sent me running.

I never gave much thought who her biological father was, until Ford and Jameson charged back into my life. And introduced a whole new level of stress.

Now I had to do the unthinkable...
Choose who would be my forever.

Playlist

Superman—Five for Fighting
Famous in a Small Town—Miranda Lambert
Good as You—Kane Brown
Stay with Me—Sam Smith
Girl Like You—Jason Aldean
Somewhere Other Than the Night—Garth Brooks
Chasing Cars—Snow Patrol
Eyes Closed—Halsey
Someone You Loved—Lewis Capaldi
Somebody to Love—OneRepublic
Sundown—Gordon Lightfoot

Want to keep up with all things Hollis Wynn?

*Make sure to sign up for the official
Hollis Wynn newsletter:*

http://eepurl.com/dj_Sb9

Join the Home Sweet Hollis on Facebook:

https://facebook.com/groups/homesweethollis

About the Author

Hollis Wynn is a thirty-something gypsy who lives for adventure and calls home anywhere that she lays her head. But she can't live without three things: music, books and her Yorkie Poo Boston.

Hollis has been writing stories for years and after successfully running the White Hot Reads blog, she finally gave into her passion and took the publishing leap.

When she's penning stories where life and love collide, you'll find her desk covered in empty wine glasses, gluten-free cupcake crumbs, and multiple drafts of her WIP covered in ink—pink of course.

Also By Hollis Wynn

A LOVE'S COMPLICATED SERIES

Bent

https://holliswynn.com/bent

Carrigan Castle may be broken but she's finally free. Free of the bonds holding her back. Free of her painful past. Free just to be. With the death of her mother, it's time to leave her small town behind and find her own way—even if it means letting go of her ideals.

A cross-country trip is about to take her to a brand-new life she never imagined. When Whit Barklay unexpectedly enters the picture, she begins the ride of her life—one filled with thrills and twists and turns. It's time to figure out where she belongs. It's time to find her way. Will Whit detour Carrigan from finding her true chance at happiness? Or will he be her North Star, pointing her to a better life with him?

One cross-country train ride to a brand-new life.

One man she never expected.

One relationship she's too scared to begin.

One risk she may not be willing to take...

Unless he can show her she's only bent and not broken.

Breathe
https://holliswynn.com/breathe

Once, it seemed my life was perfect. I had everything I thought I wanted. Then in one fell swoop, it all came crashing down. Suddenly, I don't have a fiancé *or* an apartment. If none of that was real, I'll have to figure out who I am and what I want all over again. Thank goodness I have my friends by my side.

Matt Greenstone was always one of them, a buddy who could make me smile when I frowned. But out of nowhere, there's a new feeling growing with him. A feeling that's thrilling and terrifying all at once. Something unmistakable is happening between us, and my freshly wounded heart can't help but worry about the fall. I've been down this road before, but Matt just might be different.

He makes me laugh.

He makes me smile.

He makes my heart beat faster every time I see him.

He could be my new beginning...

If I can remember to just breathe.

Crash
https://holliswynn.com/crashing-into-love

Sutton Sterling is a Capricorn through and through. A stubborn workaholic some may call pessimistic, Sutton doesn't have time to search for the roses between the thorns of potential relationships. Besides, her horoscopes never point her in the direction of love anyway. Until the day she reads one with a fresh perspective and decides to take a chance at romance and her future.

Baker Hayes has one cardinal rule—no interoffice dating. When he started working with Sutton, he considered disregarding his own boundaries. Baker accepted his role in the friend-zone but the day he happened upon Sutton's online dating blog, he's ready to start breaking some rules.

Does Sutton's horoscope decide her fate or will she and Baker go crashing into love?

Shameless Stranger (A Cocky Hero Club Novel)
https://holliswynn.com/shameless-stranger

Most people have two lives–the one they actually live and the one they dream of. For me, it's before and after. I was living my dream and loving every minute of it. It only took an instant for everything to come crashing down. Now, instead of being the center of attention, I try to hide in plain sight. Instead of champagne and parties, I have my coffee and my journal. And that's how I like it.

Until Benton Riggs enters the picture. I'm immediately drawn to him and his secrets- the main one being his Jekyll & Hyde personalities.

Mr. Push-and-Pull takes me on quiet romantic dates all over the city. Not only that, he owns half the places we go to. But just when I'm opening up to him, he pushes me away. It's infuriating—and a little addicting.

I'm falling in love with an enigma… and sometimes the truth doesn't set you free at all.